No More Hitting

By Maria Maysen

Illustrated by
Laura Logan

SCHOLASTIC INC.

For J and W and D, my most favorite hula dancers
—M.M.

For Henry & Josephine, with love
—L.L.

ISBN 978-0-545-56901-9

12 11 10 9 8 7 6 5 4 3 2   13 14 15 16 17 18/0

Printed in the U.S.A.   40
First printing, September 2013

Cubby is a happy little lion cub with an unhappy little problem.

When Cheetah zooms into the sunniest spot just as Cubby is about to curl up . . .
THWACK!

When Giraffe wants to play superhero but Cubby wants to play underwater aliens . . .
BONK!

And when Elephant uses her long elephant trunk
to scoop up all the glitter at craft time . . . BOP!

Cubby's mom says, "Paws are for hugging, Cubby."

Cubby's teacher says, "We don't hit, Cubby, not ever."

And Cubby's friends say, "OUCH!"

Cubby doesn't mean to hit, but when he feels
mad from the tip of his nose to the tip of his tail,
he doesn't know what else to do.

One Saturday morning, Cubby and Mommy walk to the playground. That's where Cubby sees something wonderful. A NEW SWING!

A supercool, shiny new swing, and Cubby knows it would swing him up to the clouds.

But Cubby isn't the only one who wants to swing up to the clouds. Just as Cubby gets ready to jump on, someone else gets there first!

BONK!

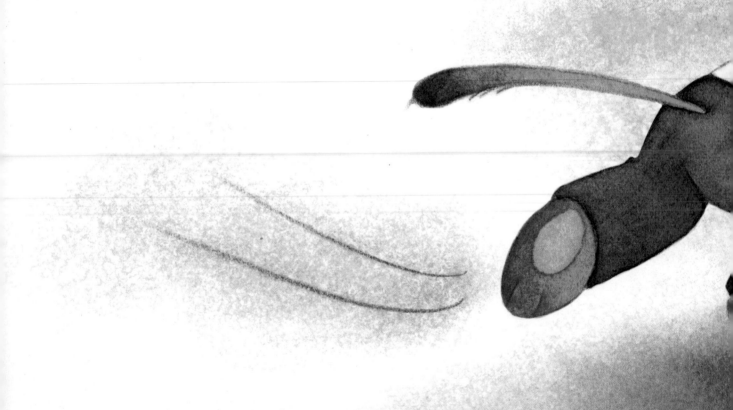

"Hey!" Cubby says. "It's my turn!"
"Nuh-uh," says Tiger. "I was here first."

"Not fair!" says Cubby. He begins to tug on the swing's rope.
But Tiger is too fast for him.

Cubby is so angry that he feels hot from the tip of his nose to the tip of his tail. He is so mad he can't talk. And that means . . . THWACK!

Cubby hits Tiger, right on her little nose.

Tiger wails, "Owie!"

Cubby's mom scolds, "Cubby!"

And Cubby pouts. "My turn!"

It isn't his turn for long. "Time to sit out," says Cubby's mom.

Just then, Cubby notices someone
new at the playground.

A monkey swings across the jungle gym.
Wow! He's the best swinger ever!

But when Monkey gets to the end
of the bars, there is a problem.

Cubby watches as Monkey becomes angry
from the tip of his nose to the tip of his tail.

Cubby is sure that Monkey is going to pop Rhino, but something funny happens. Monkey does a silly little wiggle, jumps three times, and then gently taps Rhino on the shoulder.

"Can you please move?" he asks.
And Rhino moves!

"Wow!" Cubby says, running over to Monkey after his time-out. "That was amazing! How did you do that?"

"Do what?" asks Monkey. "Swing from the bars? I'm a monkey—it's what I do!"

"No," said Cubby, "how did you keep from hitting Rhino?
I could tell you were really, really super mad."

"I *was* really, really super mad!" says Monkey. "But hitting would hurt Rhino, and it would mean I had to sit out. So I did the No-Hit-Hula instead!"

"The what?" asks Cubby.

"The No-Hit-Hula!" says Monkey. "You just clap your paws, or wiggle your tail, or hop in a circle. Just do something until you feel not-so-angry and you can use your words instead of your paws. You should try it!"

"Maybe," says Cubby, but he doesn't seem sure.

Cubby and Monkey play together for the rest of the day. When it is time to go, the new friends run for the gate. Both of them want to be the one to open it first!

"I was here first!" they yell at the same time.

Cubby is mad from the tip of his nose to the tip of his tail. Monkey is, too. They glare at each other, and just when it looks as if they are both about to bop . . .

Cubby claps his paws . . . Monkey wiggles his tail.
And then they hop around in a circle at the same time!

They're doing the No-Hit-Hula!

Cubby and Monkey hula and laugh until they forget about opening the gate.

And then they open it together.

After that, Cubby claps, wiggles, or hops every time he feels like hitting. When Cubby doesn't hit, his friends want to play with him because they won't get bopped, popped, or bonked. And no bonking means Cubby won't have to sit out.

Cubby loves the No-Hit-Hula. And he isn't the only one!

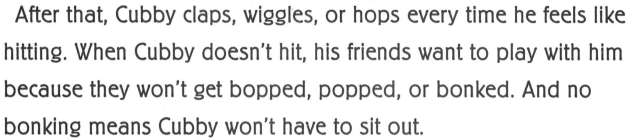